YO, JOE!

Welcome to the G.I. Joe Team. You are about to become the newest member of this top-secret antiterrorist fighting squad.

Your code name: Commando

Your major talent: To think fast—and move even faster!

Your assignment: Spy mission leader

A special G.I. Joe squad is about to go into action. The mission will not be an easy one. As team leader, it will be up to you to make sure it's a *successful* one!

Follow the directions at the bottom of each page. Then make your decision about what to do next.

If you make the right decisions, the G.I. Joe Team will score a triumph over the terrorist forces of COBRA Command, and you will be recognized as a hero. If you make the wrong choices, you'll wish you never signed up with the G.I. Joe Team.

Good luck, soldier. Take command of your special squad on page 1.

G.I. JOE

OPERATION: MINDBENDER

BY R. L. STINE

BALLANTINE BOOKS • NEW YORK

RLI: VL: Grades 5 + up

      IL: Grades 6 + up

Library of Congress Catalog Card Number: 86-90925

ISBN 0-345-33786-7

Interior Design by Gene Siegel
Editorial Services by Parachute Press, Inc.

Manufactured in the United States of America

First Edition: September 1986

Illustrated by David Henderson
Cover Art by Hector Garrido

FIND YOUR FATE™

#9

G.I. JOE

OPERATION: MINDBENDER

Slap!

The sound causes you to drop your sniper rifle. Instantly, you grab it up from the marshy ground. You spin around, finger on the trigger, to see what made that slapping noise.

"Relax, Commando," Leatherneck tells you with a frown. "That was just me slapping a mosquito. You're a little nervous, aren't you?"

"Sure I'm nervous," you admit, lowering the rifle. You peer through the tangled forest of trees. "We've been on this island for four hours, and all we've seen are mosquitoes! And where are Airtight and Beach Head? They were supposed to scout up ahead and then report back. Why aren't they back?"

Leatherneck scowls and wipes the sweat from his thick mustache. "You want my opinion?"

"No," you say, grinning. "But I'm sure I'm going to hear it anyway."

Leatherneck ignores your joke. He always does. "I think Hawk is gettin' soft in the head now that they made him a big-shot general. I think he sent us to this stupid mosquito-trap island for nothin'!"

Is Leatherneck right? Turn to page 6.

1

"If this ain't the lowest of the low," Leatherneck grumbles, glaring angrily at Airtight and Beach Head. "First I have mosquitoes using my head for a landing field. Then I get sneak-attacked by my own so-called buddies. I never shoulda left Nebraska!"

"Glad you're cheering up," you tell him.

"What are we gonna do with these traitors?" he growls.

"They're not traitors," you say firmly. "Something happened to them on the other side of the island. We have to find out what it was."

Leatherneck begins to brighten for the first time since you landed. "You mean we might have a little fightin' to do before we leave this island paradise?" He almost smiles and holds up his rifle.

"Hey—that isn't standard issue," you say, noticing the rifle for the first time. It's a 45-caliber Thompson M-1. "Where'd you get that little item, Leatherneck?"

"Souvenir of 'Nam," he says quietly. "It'll do 700 rounds a minute. Might come in handy."

"It might," you reply. "But the first thing we're gonna do is set up camp and wait right here. I've got a hunch that whatever was done to our two friends is bound to wear off soon. When it does, maybe they'll be able to lead us back to where they were."

Go on to page 3.

2

You set up camp and wait uncomfortably in the hot tropical forest, keeping close watch on Airtight and Beach Head. Finally, after three hours, Beach Head looks up at you and asks, "Hey, Commando—why am I tied up like this?"

"You and Airtight attacked us," you tell him, seeing that his eyes seem to be clear again.

Airtight looks up. "C'mon, guy," he says, shaking his head as if to clear the cobwebs. "I've done some pretty weird things in my day, but I've never attacked my own buddies."

"I've got the sore jaw to prove it," you tell him. "Maybe you two are comin' out of whatever scrambled your brains."

"Their brains were scrambled when we landed here," Leatherneck mutters, fingering his rifle.

"You've been breathin' too much swamp gas, Leatherneck!" Airtight yells angrily. "There's nothin' wrong with *our* brains! We don't need a hardheaded Marine to tell us—"

"Stow it!" you yell, pushing a furious Leatherneck back. "We don't have time for this. Listen, you two—do you remember what happened to you on the other side of the island?"

"We were captured," Beach Head says. His voice is as flat and emotionless as always. He never gets riled, not even now, after this bizarre episode.

"Captured by whom?" you ask.

"By COBRA Crimson Guards," he replies.

Turn to page 28.

3

You lead the G.I. Joe unit over the burning remains of the white fence and barrel through the entrance of Zartan's secret fortress. More Crimson Guards leap out to stop you. Weapon-fire echoes through the low corridors. The only other sound is the thud of your boots against the concrete floor.

"YO, JOE!" you yell.

Zartan must know you're here by now, must hear your cries of triumph as you batter your way through his guards. But where is he?

You force open a large double door at the end of the corridor, sounds of fighting still behind you. The door falls with a crack and you rush inside, finger on the trigger, ready to shoot anything that moves.

"Stop right there!" a high-pitched voice shrieks.

You stop. You have found Zartan. His eyes are wide with excitement beneath the black-and-white makeup that covers his face.

"Don't make another move—if you value your leader's life!" Zartan screams.

What does he mean? You look to his left. Two people are tied together with ropes. Their feet are bound, and they are guarded by four CGs with pistols held to their heads.

You can't believe your eyes. The two prisoners are Hawk and Lady Jaye!

Go on to page 5.

4

"Throw down your weapons and they won't get hurt!" Zartan shrieks, an evil grin on his face.

"Please—do as he says!" Lady Jaye, her voice trembling, pleads with you.

"Do as he says—or he'll kill us both!" Hawk says. "Throw down your weapons, Commando. That's an order."

"We don't throw down our weapons for anyone!" Leatherneck screams.

You spin around and motion for him to shut up. This isn't the time for hot words. You have only seconds to decide what to do.

Is this some sort of trick of Zartan's? You don't have time to think—you've got to act.

Throw down your weapons? Turn to page 44.
Keep fighting? Turn to page 72.

A beautiful red macaw soars from a tree limb above your heads. The rhythmic flapping of its wide wings is the only sound to break the stillness in this South Pacific island forest.

"You know the official word," you tell Leatherneck. "Army spy planes picked up signs of some sort of military activity on this island. Maybe COBRA is up to something. Maybe it isn't COBRA. Hawk thought it was important enough to send us here to check it out."

Leatherneck scowls again. It is the natural expression of his face. You realize you've never seen this tough old Marine smile.

"Hawk just wants to impress the cigar-chompers in D.C.," he says, frowning. "Maybe they'll pin another shiny star on his chest—if there's room." He swats another mosquito.

"Hey, Leatherneck," you say, "you're not bitter, are you?"

He glares at you. "Bitter? Listen, kid, I was born suckin' lemons!"

You start to reply, but you hear other sounds. "Hit the ground!" you tell him. "Someone's coming!"

Turn to page 52.

"That's very kind of you, Buzzer, but we really don't need help," you say, taking a step back, trying to signal to your companions to be ready for a fight.

But there's no need to signal. They're ready.

Monkeywrench pulls a grenade from his weapons belt. "Let's blow 'em up, Buzzer," he says. "Just for laughs, okay?"

Ripper pull a pistol from his belt. Buzzer starts to laugh. "Okay. Let's give 'em a little loyalty test," he says.

The Dreadnoks move in.

Quickly, you try to figure out the best way to fight back.

Suddenly, shots ring out. . . .

Turn to page 25.

You leave the unconscious Dreadnoks behind and roar off toward Zartan's headquarters. But you don't get far from the clearing.

Your path is quickly cut off by heavily armed COBRA Assault System Pods (ASPs), which block your way. Each jet-propelled pod carries a Crimson Guard in its cockpit. In the sky above you, two COBRA F.A.N.G.s (Fully Armed Negator Gyro-copters) appear, their 300-millimeter cannons aimed down at you.

Even Leatherneck, riding behind you on your borrowed chopper, realizes you don't stand a chance. He grudgingly lowers his M-1. You wait for the Crimson Guards to close in....

Turn to page 50.

"Let's get Zartan—before he can call for reinforcements!" you yell to Leatherneck.

"I never liked that black-and-white makeup he wears," Leatherneck yells as you fight your way to the door at the far end of the lab. "There's only one other animal I know that's black-and-white like him—a skunk!"

You jam the butt of your rifle into the pit of a Crimson Guard's stomach, and he drops to the floor with a shocked gasp. You pull open the door and run down the dark corridor. You hear running footsteps several yards ahead of you—Zartan's.

You see him running at full speed through another doorway. Sunlight pours in as the door opens. Zartan is running across the sand now, toward the small dock where the powerboat is tied. You are running faster, faster, trying to close the gap. You know you've got to stop him before he gets into the boat and escapes.

Turn to page 77.

Leatherneck starts to tumble forward. How will you ever get him back to the Skystriker? Then, suddenly, he swings both fists up, catching Zartan beneath the chin. Zartan is too startled to cry out. He slumps backward to the pavement, unconscious.

"Let's go!" you cry, and you and Leatherneck make a run for the ramp to the Skystriker. You reach the ramp and look back. Zandar is frantically trying to revive his brother.

"Get 'er up! Get 'er up!" you cry to the pilot as Zandar opens fire.

Minutes later, you are airborne. You activate the radio and contact the Pit. "We're in a little trouble here," you say. "I think we could use some help, if you can spare it."

Can help get to you in time? Black-and-crimson COBRA Rattlers suddenly fill the sky. The Skystriker swerves and dives, narrowly avoiding their deadly combat rockets. The sky glows red from rockets and missile fire.

"We can't dodge 'em all afternoon!" Leatherneck yells as a rocket explodes near the plane, causing it to shake like a washing machine in spin cycle. "We're a little outnumbered!"

You man the guns and begin blasting away at the high-speed Rattler attack jets.

KAA-BLAAAAAM! A Rattler leaves a trail of flame as it plummets to the ground.

"You're right," you say glumly. "I don't know how much longer we can hold out...."

Turn to page 82.

You don't have time to think about the small crafts now. A Crimson Guard slams the butt of his pistol into your ribs. You cry out, stumble toward the rail. He turns his attention to Beach Head, who casually finishes him off with a powerful strike to the throat. Trying to catch your breath, you look toward the approaching crafts.

They're G.I. Joe WHALES! Some of your buddies are riding the waves on the powerful and well-armed hovercrafts. You watch as COBRA Commander's cruiser disappears over the misty gray horizon. COBRA Commander has decided to avoid any trouble.

And now you see that Zartan has made the same decision. Leaving the scene of the fight, he runs toward the lifeboats in the bow. "After him!" Leatherneck yells, shoving a CG out of his way.

"Let him go! We'll get him soon enough!" you call to Leatherneck. "He won't have anywhere to go—if we demolish his little fortress on shore."

Zartan lowers himself down to the water in a small lifeboat. You turn your attention to the G.I. Joe WHALE hovercrafts that have surrounded the ship....

Turn to page 64.

You stumble backward in pain, too stunned even to utter a cry of protest. The sky spins above your eyes. When you can focus again, you see that Beach Head has swung the butt of his rifle into Leatherneck's stomach.

Leatherneck groans and lurches to the ground.

What is going on here? Why are your buddies attacking you? You decide there's only one way to find out. You're going to have to defeat them first!

Your jaw still throbbing with pain, you leap onto Beach Head's back and push him to the ground. He rolls free and dives at you, but he leaps right into your fist. You hesitate for a second. You can't believe you're battling your friend. But then you let him have it, again, again. He slumps to the ground, dazed and groaning.

You turn and see that Leatherneck has managed to subdue Airtight. Airtight's nose is bleeding. Leatherneck appears to be trying to twist his arm off. "Airtight, if this is one of your idiot practical jokes, I still ain't gonna say I'm sorry," he growls.

"Knock it off! Knock if off!" you cry, rubbing your aching jaw. "What's *with* you guys, anyway?"

Turn to page 24.

The Crimson Guards shove the four of you into Dr. Mindbender's lab. You look around the long room, surprised to find so much machinery and wiring in this primitive structure. Sunlight pours through a large window overlooking the ocean.

Mindbender appears, a short, bald man in a white lab coat. At first glance he looks like a dentist, which he was. But the evil glare of his eyes and the curled sneer of his lips beneath his broad black mustache quickly change your mind. Mindbender is no mere dentist.

Mindbender eyes each of you slowly. He doesn't say a word but gestures toward a tall metal-and-chrome machine at the far end of the lab.

A few seconds later, thanks to the Crimson Guards, all four of you are attached to the machine.

Turn to page 78.

"Zartan!" you cry.

Leatherneck raises his M-1 and prepares to fire.

"I've caught Dr. Mindbender, sir," Zartan says, shoving the scowling Dr. Mindbender toward you. "He was heading for the powerboat on the dock. He put up a pretty good fight, but not good enough to get away from me!"

"Good going, Zartan," you say, unable to hold back a grin. "Take Mindbender prisoner," you tell Airtight and Beach Head. "I'll put in a good word for you back at HQ for this, Zartan," you say.

Zartan salutes you. "Thank you, sir," he says. "My men and I will help guide you back to your vehicles now."

You look at your teammates and shrug. Apparently, one of the electronic rays from the exploding mind-altering machine must have struck Zartan. He is now as loyal to the G.I. Joe Team as any one of you.

"We're gonna have one problem when we get back to the Pit," you tell Leatherneck as you lead them all away.

"What's that?" he asks.

"No one is going to believe any of this!"

THE END

"This ship belongs to us!" Leatherneck whispers. You appreciate his enthusiasm. But you realize you're going to need a break if your plan is to succeed.

At that moment, COBRA Commander's cruiser comes into view on the horizon. This is the break you need. Zartan, the captain, and the guards turn to look at the approaching ship, its red-and-black COBRA flag flying high above its prow.

"NOW!" you scream, and you leap onto one of the Crimson Guards. Both of you tumble to the deck. You reach for his automatic pistol, but his hand reaches the holster first. He pulls out the pistol and raises it toward your head....

Turn to page 30.

Not a word is spoken. The Crimson Guards take away your rifles. They drag Airtight and Beach Head to their feet. Then they begin marching the four of you through the island forest.

Overhead, birds cry in alarm. The orange sun sends rays of blistering heat through the openings between the palm tree fronds.

You are surrounded by the soldiers. You cannot escape.

The trees thin out. You find yourselves walking down a gentle, sandy dune. At the bottom of the dune, you see the Pacific. Built right at the water's edge is a long, low building with a dock. A powerboat bearing the COBRA insignia bobs in the water beside the small dock.

A tall radio transmitter juts from the flat roof of the building. Several CGs guard the entrance. This is definitely some sort of headquarters—but whose?

You don't have to wait long to find out the answer to that question. The CGs push you into a large, low chamber inside the building. Zartan steps into the room, grinning under the black-and-white makeup that always hides his face. He glances at you quickly and then begins talking to the leader of the CGs.

What will you do now?

....

Try to grab a rifle from a CG while Zartan is distracted and fight your way out? Turn to page 20.

Wait until you see what Zartan is up to on this island fortress? Turn to page 56.

17

With lightning speed, you pull open the door to the tunnel. A high wave of ocean water slams into the room, sweeping the Crimson Guards off their feet, swirling through the lab.

"No! No! Stop it!" Zartan screams.

You leap at him, but he scrambles out of your grasp. He falls facedown into the rising water, picks himself up, and runs across the lab.

You and Leatherneck go after him. But three figures move quickly to block your way. "Oh no," you mutter, recognizing the three thugs at once. They are Zartan's loyal followers, Ripper, Buzzer, and Monkeywrench—the Dreadnoks.

"I think we're about to have a bit of a set-to, mates," Monkeywrench says, a thick-lipped smile across his loutish face. He raises a four-foot length of chain and swings it like a whip at Leatherneck. Leatherneck makes a grab for the chain, misses, and slides forward into the water. Ripper batters the fallen Marine on the back of the head with his pistol butt.

You look around. Zartan watches eagerly. You are alone now. The Dreadnoks, grinning, move in for the kill....

Go on to page 19.

18

Suddenly, the door at the far end of the lab crashes to the floor. Everyone turns around. You take advantage of the distraction to leap away from the Dreadnoks, and grab a fresh sniper rifle from a fallen Crimson Guard.

"Hey, Commando, did you call for the cavalry?"

Hawk and his squad enter the lab with their rifles blasting. Astonished CGs fall to the wet floor. The Dreadnoks show their true nature by panicking and running out the tunnel door—but the water rushing through the broken tunnel pushes them back into the lab.

"Hey—I coulda handled this!" you tell Hawk, pushing the tunnel door closed.

"Sure thing," he says. "But when we didn't hear from you at the Pit for nearly twenty-four hours, I figured maybe you could use a few friendly faces—and rifles."

"Yeah, well—" you start to say. But Hawk can't hear you. He's blasting away at a group of CGs. Suddenly, Zartan reappears—and jams the barrel of an automatic machine rifle into his back. Then he shoves Hawk toward the console and forces a pair of headphones over his ears.

"Throw the switch! Throw the switch!" Zartan screams.

You've got to rescue Hawk before Dr. Mindbender's ray can enter his brain. But how?

....

Try to free him from Zartan's grasp. Turn to page 55.

Blast the console? Turn to page 35.

19

Zartan, his dark hair flowing down to his shoulders, has his back to you. The Crimson Guards seem to relax, having completed their mission by bringing you here.

You get Leatherneck's attention and signal with your eyes that this might be a good time to try to free yourselves. He gives you a quick V signal.

You leap forward, reaching for the handle of one of the Crimson Guards' rifles.

"Stop!" a voice calls out. Hands grab you from behind and spin you around before you can grasp the rifle.

It is Airtight. He lands a solid punch on your jaw that sends you sprawling to the floor.

As you go down you see that Beach Head has taken Leatherneck by surprise.

You have been stopped by your own buddies. They are still loyal to Zartan.

Why are all these CGs working for Zartan? What is he doing on this island? And why are your two teammates under his spell?

These are questions you will never be able to answer, for Zartan has signaled his loyal troops to finish you off. And they move quickly to obey....

THE END

Zartan and the Crimson Guards lead you and your buddies outside. The aqua-blue ocean water sparkles in the late afternoon sun. Palm trees, silent and unmoving, line the beach beyond Zartan's headquarters. The small motorboat bobs up and down on the choppy blue waters.

"Looks like a picture postcard, don't it?" Leatherneck growls. "Havin' a lovely time. Wish you were here instead of me. Ha ha!"

"Leatherneck, this is no time for you to develop a sense of humor," you tell him.

A Crimson Guard gives you a shove. The four of you are pushed along the small dock and forced down into the speedboat. CGs climb in behind you. Zartan himself takes the wheel.

"I want you out of the way," he tells you. "COBRA Commander will be here soon to see the work I am doing. Ha ha! I can't wait for him to experience Dr. Mindbender's ray! Then even *he* will be loyal to Zartan!"

You stare into his makeup-shadowed eyes. They are the eyes of a madman!

He steers the speedboat over the choppy blue waters to the small battle cruiser. You are all hoisted aboard. "Hold them here until COBRA Commander has safely arrived," Zartan commands. "I don't want anything to spoil his arrival. Ha ha! Then, after he has docked, toss these four clowns overboard!"

....

Turn to page 63.

21

Holding on to the side of the cockpit, you reach one hand up, grab at the pistol, miss, grab again. Dr. Mindbender squeezes the trigger.

The bullet whistles past your face.

You grab the gun. You and your opponent battle for it as you cling to the side of the chopper. He slaps the gun out of your hand. You make a desperate grab for it. You miss. You and Mindbender watch it fall into the sparkling blue waters below.

In your attempt to get control of the gun, your grip loosens on the side of the cockpit. You slip, grab hold. Mindbender struggles to pry your hands from the craft.

"Let go! Let go! You're pulling the chopper down!" Mindbender screams.

You look down. He's right. You are tilting the chopper so that it cannot stay up. Lower, lower, you are dropping toward the churning blue waters.

"Get off! Get off!" Mindbender screams. "You're pulling us both down!" He slams his fists onto your hands, desperately trying to loosen your grip.

"Oh no!" you cry as you slip off the side of the chopper and begin to fall. . . .

Turn to page 37.

Though they are beaten, Beach Head and Airtight continue to struggle, and you are forced to tie them up. They pull against the ropes, refusing to answer any of your questions. You get the feeling that they don't really recognize you.

Have they been brainwashed?

"I think we have a problem here," you say thoughtfully.

"Tell me about it," Leatherneck mumbles.

They call you Commando because of your ability to act under pressure with lightning speed. Now you've got to make a decision about what to do next. How will you deal with this problem and still complete your mission?

Should you try to force Beach Head and Airtight to retrace their steps? If you follow them back to where they were scouting, you might find out what happened to them.

Or do you think it's smarter to radio the Pit at once, let Hawk know what has happened—and ask for reinforcements?

Or would it be best to fly your two confused buddies back to the Pit for immediate medical care? It's up to you!

....

Go back to where Beach Head and Airtight were scouting? Turn to page 2.

Radio the Pit for reinforcements? Turn to page 47.

Fly Beach Head and Airtight back to the Pit? Turn to page 48.

24

You hit the soft ground as the shots whistle over your head. Into the clearing come Flint, Roadblock, and a squad of G.I. Joe infantrymen, their rifles blazing.

"Think we ought to hit the road, mates!" cries Buzzer, trying to start up his chopper.

"Don't let them get away!" you cry. "They'll go right to Zartan!"

You leap onto Buzzer's back and pull him off his chopper. Leatherneck and Airtight knock the other two thugs to the ground. "One move and you'll eat dirt!" Leatherneck yells as Beach Head holds a sniper rifle on them.

"Hey, Commando," Flint calls to you, with a wide grin. "I thought maybe we'd join the picnic."

"It's no picnic," you tell him seriously.

"We know," Flint says, pulling his green beret into place. "Our spy planes picked up more activity on the island. That's why we were sent in as backup. What next?"

"On to Zartan's little beach house," you say. "But here's the question: Do we go in with guns blazing? Or do we try to trick Zartan into thinking that Airtight and Beach Head are still loyal to him—and that they've captured us and are bringing us in for brainwashing?"

Which strategy do you choose?

....

Attack the fortress with guns blazing? Turn to page 60.

Try to get to Zartan by tricking him? Turn to page 58.

A few minutes later, Leatherneck comes back into the cabin and sits down next to you. "What are you so jumpy about?" you ask him.

"I'm tellin' you, there's somethin' wrong here," Leatherneck insists. "Here, I'll show ya." He calls back to Beach Head, "Hey, Beach Head, whatever happened to your little sister? You told me she'd write to me, remember?"

"How should I know?" Beach Head says angrily. "I can't make her write if she doesn't want to—can I?"

"See?" Leatherneck whispers. "Beach Head doesn't have a sister. There's somethin' weird here."

"Their brains were completely scrambled back on that island," you tell him. "The poor guys don't know *what* they're saying. I guess...." You stop talking, distracted because the plane is starting to land.

You look up. Airtight and Beach Head are standing beside your seat. They've freed themselves somehow. And they've picked up guns from the back cabin of the plane. "Fasten your seatbelts," Airtight says, shoving the barrel of his pistol in your face. "We wouldn't want anything to happen to you—*would* we!"

Go on to page 27.

The jet pulls down for a landing. The cabin is jolted as the wheels touch down. But Airtight and Beach Head hold tightly to their guns, which are trained on you and Leatherneck.

"Listen, you guys. We're going to get you to the doc. You're gonna be fine," you tell them quietly, soothingly.

"That won't be necessary," Airtight says in a voice you've never heard before. He and his companion pull off holographic masks.

"Zartan!" you cry, recognizing the COBRA master of disguise.

"Allow me to introduce my brother," Zartan says, pleased by the success of their disguises. "This is Zandar. We make rather good G.I. Joe Team members, don't you think?"

Leatherneck snarls and tries to grab the pistol from Zartan's hand. Zartan shoves the gun barrel into Leatherneck's face. "Don't be stupid," he tells him. "There is plenty of time for you to die."

"Your little disguise won't get you anywhere," you tell Zartan.

"It already has," Zartan says, almost gleefully. "Have we not landed at the secret headquarters of the G.I. Joe Team? You two fools have taken us right to it. We carry radio transmitters. In a few minutes, COBRA Rattlers will fill the skies. Your precious headquarters is doomed!"

Turn to page 41.

"COBRA? COBRA's on this island?" Leatherneck cries, raising his rifle.

"Well...not exactly," Beach Head says. "Hey, Commando—can't you untie us now?"

You glance at Leatherneck. He shrugs. "Okay," you say, bending over to remove the ropes from their wrists. "Keep talking while I get you outta these."

"We came to a headquarters right at the edge of the water on the far side of the island," Beach Head continues. "We were about to come back and get you, Commando. But we were captured by COBRA CGs. They forced us to go inside this place. It's all made of wood, but it's built like a fortress, and it's pretty big. Now, here's the funny part—"

"Yeah. *Real* funny," Airtight says sarcastically.

Beach Head ignores him and goes on. "The COBRA Crimson Guards were the ones who captured us. But they weren't there workin' for COBRA Commander. They were all loyal to Zartan!"

Zartan, master of a million disguises and personalities, has long been one of COBRA Commander's most deadly henchmen. Has he decided to strike out on his own?

"That's not the end of the story," Beach Head says calmly. "Wait—it gets even better—"

Turn to page 86.

"Zartan's headed toward the dock!" you yell. "After him! We'll come back and take care of this lab after we've captured him!"

You and the rest of the G.I. Joe unit run past the giant console to the back exit of the lab. Suddenly, there's a flash of magenta which quickly pales to yellow and then to white. You feel a strong tingling, a jolt of electricity.

You have all run right through Dr. Mindbender's mind-altering ray!

"Halt!" you command, and everyone pulls up behind you, lowering their weapons. "Let's go see if Zartan needs our help."

You run after him. Zartan turns to face you.

"May we assist you, sir, in getting your boat started?" you ask, saluting your leader.

He smiles. "No thank you, soldier. From the looks of things, I won't be needing to leave in this boat after all. Not since I have such good, loyal soldiers here to protect me."

"Thank you, sir," you say. "We will all await your further commands."

THE END

You roll off the Crimson Guard and spin away as his pistol goes off. You leap to your feet, step forward, and kick the gun from his hand. He howls in pain as your boot crushes his hand.

You scramble for the pistol and grab it up from the deck. Still holding his wounded hand, the CG lurches toward you. You let him have it with his own gun. He topples over the side and plunges into the blue waters.

You turn and see Leatherneck raise a CG over his head. "Let's change your name to Fish Food!" he yells, tossing the struggling enemy overboard.

Airtight ducks as Zartan fires one of the Crimson Guards' automatic pistols at him. The bullets pound into the deck, just missing. Airtight tackles Zartan. They roll around on the deck, pummeling each other frantically, Airtight using his head as a battering ram against Zartan's chest.

Suddenly, you hear the roar of engines outside the ship. You look out. On the horizon, not far from COBRA Commander's cruiser, you see small crafts approaching.

Is Cobra Commander sending his forces to rescue Zartan?

Turn to page 12.

"Let 'em come," you tell your companions. "If we can trick the Dreadnoks into thinking we're loyal followers of their beloved Zartan, they'll lead us right to him!"

"I don't like standin' here and waitin' for them to pick us off. We're sittin' ducks!" Leatherneck protests.

"Quack, quack," says Airtight, showing the kind of wit he's known for. Leatherneck glares at him. Airtight grins back.

The three Dreadnoks roar up on their cycles and begin to ride around you in smaller and smaller circles, howling gleefully. Finally, they pull to a stop and cut their engines. "Well, I'll be a wallaby's uncle!" Monkeywrench exclaims, fingering the belt of grenades he wears across his chest. "Look what we 'ave 'ere, mates!"

"I ain't seen nothin' like this since I visited the zoo back in Sidney," Buzzer says, spitting on your boots, his face twisted into a sneer of contempt.

You raise your fist in a salute. "Long live Zartan!" you cry. "We are soldiers in *his* army now."

The three thugs look at each other in confusion. "Maybe these are the blokes who got their brains repaired in Dr. Mindbender's machine," Ripper says finally.

"We are soldiers in Zartan's army," you say. "Zartan is our only leader now."

Will the Dreadnoks believe you?

Go on to page 33.

Buzzer pulls a filthy red handkerchief from his jeans pocket and wipes the sweat off his forehead. Despite the tropical heat, all three of them are wearing black leather biking gear. What a tribute to their intelligence, you think to yourself. Will they be smart enough to see through your plan?

"So...you blokes are loyal to Zartan now?" Buzzer asks, raising the buzz saw that is always at his side.

"We are proud soldiers in his army," Airtight says, his eyes glazed over as if in a hypnotic spell.

Buzzer rubs his stubbled chin, thinking hard. "Then tell me and me mates this—what are you doing out here, walkin' around in the trees?"

You realize you've got to think quickly. Buzzer has asked a good question. You've got to give him a good reply.

"There are more G.I. Joe Team members on the island," you tell him. "Our plan was to ambush them and take them to Zartan."

Buzzer stares into your eyes, trying to decide if you're telling the truth. Finally, he grins and says, "Good. Me and me mates'll join you."

This is the reply you didn't want to hear! What do you do now?

Turn to page 7.

You dive for a Crimson Guard's knees. He lets out a cry of pain as you push him over and his head hits the concrete floor. With one quick motion you take away his rifle and leap to your feet.

Another CG leaps at you. You greet him with a volley of rifle fire. You and Leatherneck fight your way to the far exit. "Hey—look!" Leatherneck yells, pointing.

You turn around and see that Airtight and Beach Head have turned their rifles on the CGs who are pursuing you. The effects of Dr. Mindbender's ray seem to have worn off.

You see Dr. Mindbender creeping along the far wall, trying to make his escape from the lab. He ducks as stray bullets fly in his direction.

You must decide what to do next.

You're sure that Zartan will soon return with reinforcements—unless you stop him first.

Go after Zartan? Turn to page 9.
Go after Dr. Mindbender? Turn to page 79.

You realize you have only seconds to destroy the console. You pick up the length of chain Monkeywrench dropped on the floor. Grasping one end tightly, you swing it at Zartan. It catches the machine rifle and pulls it from his hand.

You dive for the gun, grab it up, and turn it on Mindbender's machine. The console explodes in a blast of orange and purple flame.

Hawk dives free. Zartan is hit in the back by a metal chunk of debris. He cries out, staggers to his feet, and commands his Crimson Guards to attack.

"Close in on them! We still have them outnumbered!" he shouts to the Crimson Guards.

But they make no move to follow Zartan's orders.

By blowing up the console, you've erased Mindbender's effect on their minds. The CGs realize that they have been disloyal to their true leader—COBRA Commander.

Zartan realizes this at the same moment you do. He turns, runs, bolts through the door, and flees across the beach, followed by Dr. Mindbender. The CGs chase after them.

"They'll never escape," you tell Hawk.

"I think we've done pretty well for one day," he says. "Let's move on outta here!"

He doesn't have to ask you twice!

THE END

"Hold your fire!" you order. "And keep down low!"

You wait until the onrushing Dreadnoks are only a few hundred yards away. Then the G.I. Joe Team lets loose a barrage of weapon-fire.

The startled Dreadnoks wheel up, spinning wildly in the soft dirt, their cycles careening out of control. Ripper raises a pistol and takes aim. But Leatherneck's M-1 blasts the cycle out from under him, and his pistol flies into the trees.

Monkeywrench cries out as he is hit. His cycle spins and falls, trapping him beneath it.

Buzzer's cycle roars toward you. It appears that Buzzer plans to ride right *through* you! "Wait—Airtight!" you scream. But that crazy G.I. Joe, up to his old tricks, leaps onto the back of the cycle. "Can't this thing go any faster?" he yells to Buzzer.

Buzzer turns and swerves, trying to throw Airtight off. But Airtight holds on to Buzzer's back for dear life. Then Airtight strikes hard at the back of Buzzer's neck. Buzzer sprawls forward, unconscious, and Airtight flicks him off the chopper. He begins to ride in circles around the three of you, a triumphant grin spread across his face.

"Take their cycles! We'll ride the rest of the way!" Airtight yells.

Turn to page 8.

You gasp. Every muscle in your body tightens from the shock of the icy water. You sink down. You struggle to relax, to let your body adjust, to let your muscles loosen, to float, float. . . .

Breaking the surface, you look to the sky. You suck in deep breaths of air. You see the COBRA chopper hit the water—and explode.

The impact of hitting the water must have set off the bomb it carried. You spin around, trying to see clearly. The explosion sets off wave after wave. You try to stay afloat, give up, and find that it's better to swim under the rolling waves.

Soon the waters calm. You come back to the surface. There is no sign of Mindbender or his chopper.

You turn and swim to shore, pulling yourself up onto the small dock beside Zartan's low fortress.

It is silent inside. The guns have all stopped.

Warily, you creep back into the building.

What has happened?

Turn to page 88.

"What the—" Leatherneck scratches his head, bewildered. "Where'd he go?"

"Maybe he's swimming home," you say, your eyes searching the water as you try to catch your breath. The boards creak under your boots. You look down. "Hey, Leatherneck—look here. A trapdoor. Maybe—"

Before you can finish your thought, you both hear a loud hissing noise. It is a familiar sound—the sound of a lit fuse. "Explosives!" you yell.

You've got to move—*fast!*

Jump onto the boat? Turn to page 68.

Open the trapdoor and climb down to wherever it leads? Turn to page 46.

38

"No, Hawk! No!" You stare into his eyes, try to reach him, try to get through to the real Hawk, your friend, your leader.

His eyes are a blank.

He raises the machine rifle. Through the corner of your eye you see the triumphant Zartan grinning, enjoying his victory.

"So long," Hawk says flatly.

Then, suddenly, astonishingly, he spins around—

—and blasts the giant console with the machine rifle!

The console explodes, filling the room with a cloud of choking gray smoke.

When the smoke clears, Zartan is no longer grinning. He is Hawk's prisoner.

Hawk is the one doing the grinning now. And after you realize what has happened, your face also breaks out in a wide smile.

"Had you going there for a moment, didn't I?" Hawk gloats.

"No, not at all," you tell him. "I knew you were too brain-damaged for that ray to have any effect."

Hawk looks insulted. "That's the way you talk to your commanding officer?"

"Sorry," you say, still grinning. "I knew you were too brain-damaged for that ray to have any effect—*sir*!"

THE END

Rifles roar. But they aren't COBRA Crimson Guard rifles.

Flint, Roadblock, and their backup burst into the lab. The fight is over in a matter of moments. The CGs are no match for the G.I. Joe Team.

"Zartan got away in a speedboat," Flint says, staring at all the complicated wiring and machinery. "But we've got control of this place. He won't be coming back."

"Mission accomplished," you say, handing Dr. Mindbender over to him.

"My machine! My machine! Why didn't it work?" Mindbender asks, still confused.

"I can answer that," Flint says. He holds up two small glass-and-metal objects. "We found the main fuse box outside." He flips the two fuses into the air and turns to you. "We thought it would be a bit easier to stay outside and simply remove a few fuses than to come in shooting up the lab to rescue you guys, Commando."

"Easier for *you*, maybe," you say grudgingly.

Flint laughs. "I guess you're right. But a little suspense always makes for a better story—don't you agree?"

THE END

"Let's go," Zartan says, motioning with his pistol for you to get up. "Let's go take a look at your precious hidden headquarters."

"It'll be a *last* look," Zandar adds with a laugh.

With a sharp order to the pilot to remain in the craft, they force you out of the Skystriker. You step onto a small landing field.

"What the—" Zartan yells angrily, looking around. There is a small shack at the end of the landing strip, and then nothing but rolling, grassy hills as far as the eye can see. "Where are we?"

"Welcome to Pennsylvania," Leatherneck says, grinning. He turns and whispers to you. "When I got suspicious, I went up and told the pilot to land here instead of the Pit. Pretty smart, huh?"

"Yeah. Pretty smart," you agree. "But we're still dead meat."

Zartan is furious that he has been tricked. He swings the butt of his pistol into Leatherneck's stomach. Leatherneck's eyes bulge. He starts to crumble to the pavement.

You've got to decide quickly what to do.

....

Fight them and try to defeat them on this air-strip? Turn to page 84.

Try to get back into the Skystriker? Turn to page 10.

41

"Run!" you yell—but there's no need. You are both running as fast as you can, your heads lowered in this small passage, listening to the whoosh of onrushing water as it becomes a loud roar.

The water is up over your ankles and you keep running, raising your legs high, following the path of this mysterious tunnel.

The water is up to your knees. In a few seconds, you will have to start swimming. You look up at the low ceiling as you run. It won't take long for the rushing water to fill the tunnel, you realize.

"Look—a doorway!" Leatherneck yells. You've reached the end of the tunnel. He pushes open the door with his shoulder, and you run through it quickly, slamming it shut before the water can rush through.

You find yourselves back where you started—in Dr. Mindbender's lab!

"Kill them!" Zartan yells. He has had time to get his reinforcements in place. You are staring at the firing ends of more than two dozen Crimson Guard sniper rifles. . . .

Turn to page 18.

The room is silent. One of the Crimson Guards spins the chamber of his pistol as he points it at Hawk's head.

"We have no choice," you tell your comrades. "We have to drop our weapons."

"No—" Leatherneck starts to protest. But he sees that your mind is made up. He spits angrily on the floor and turns away, his face red with anger.

"Please—hurry," Lady Jaye pleads.

"Drop your weapons!" you order.

A broad smile spreads across Zartan's face as all the G.I. Joe weapons clatter to the floor. "What a touching scene!" Zartan cries. "You throw down your weapons, your only hope of defeating me, in order to save your precious leader and the lady. What a touching scene indeed. Hahaha!"

Zartan laughs loudly as the Crimson Guards step away from Hawk and Lady Jaye and rush forward to collect your rifles. The guards are laughing too.

"You fools!" Hawk cries, joining in the laughter....

Turn to page 69.

44

"Go on! Keep goin'!" Leatherneck yells, holding his shoulder. "Don't let him get away!"

You hesitate, seeing a pool of blood widen on Leatherneck's shoulder. You turn and see Mindbender running across the beach.

"Get goin', Commando," Leatherneck continues to urge. "What's the matter—you ain't seen a little scratch like this before?"

"Stay right there—" you tell Leatherneck. "Don't go back and try to mop up all the Crimson Guards with one hand." You give him a thumbs-up and take off after Mindbender.

Behind a clump of scraggly bushes near the water, Mindbender has a COBRA F.A.N.G. hidden. In seconds, he has climbed into the fully armed chopper and has activated the engine.

"You're not goin' anywhere!" you cry over the roar of the chopper's engine as it begins its vertical takeoff.

How are you going to stop Mindbender?

Try to blast the chopper with the COBRA sniper rifle you're carrying? Turn to page 67.

Grab the landing runner and pull yourself up into the chopper? Turn to page 54.

You reach down and pull open the wooden trapdoor. "Quick—" you yell to Leatherneck, "Zartan must've gone down this way!"

You both dive through the open door as quickly as you can. You find yourselves in a dark, narrow tunnel beneath the dock.

BAAARRROOOOOM!

A loud explosion shakes the walls of the tunnel. "The boat was rigged with explosives," you say, uttering a silent thank-you that you didn't choose to jump onto the boat.

"That was a close call," Leatherneck mutters, shaking his head. "Hey, what's that sound?"

It takes you a few seconds to recognize it. It's rushing water!

The explosion must have ripped a hole in the tunnel....

Turn to page 42.

"This is too weird for us to handle," you tell Leatherneck, trying to force the worry from your voice. "We were sent here to do a little scouting—not get involved in any COBRA brainwashing plot."

Leatherneck pulls the portable worldwide radio transmitter from his backpack. "Hawk'll never believe this one," he mutters, shaking his head.

"We've got to make him believe it," you say grimly. "We need some more men here. The two of us are helpless—especially if we have to keep a close watch on our own buddies!"

Leatherneck activates the radio transmitter and begins pounding out a coded radio message. He shakes his head. He starts again. You both listen.

Silence.

The silence is replaced by loud static.

Leatherneck tosses the transmitter down into the dirt in disgust.

Someone is jamming your signal with a very powerful transmitter. You can't get through to the Pit. You're on your own....

Turn to page 76.

47

"Our buddies here are seriously messed up," you say. "We've got to get them back to the Pit so the docs can check 'em out."

Leatherneck doesn't want to give up the mission, but he reluctantly agrees.

You push your two fellow teammates onto the Skystriker fighter jet, and a few minutes later the four of you are flying at supersonic speeds back to the Pit.

"Got a cigarette?" Airtight asks suddenly.

Leatherneck gives him a strange look. "I've never seen you smoke," he tells Airtight.

"Have you got one or not?" Airtight asks impatiently.

Leatherneck hands him a cigarette and lights it for him. Then he frees one hand just enough for Airtight to be able to smoke. "That's a funny way to hold a cigarette," he tells Airtight suspiciously. "Isn't that the way Russians hold their cigarettes?"

Airtight quickly moves the cigarette around in his hand. "Leave me alone," is his only reply.

Leatherneck comes up and sits beside you. "Something weird about Airtight and Beach Head," he says quietly.

"Tell me something I didn't already know," you say sarcastically.

"No—not just that they've turned traitor," he says. Then he gets up nervously and goes up front to talk to the Skystriker's pilot. . . .

Turn to page 26.

48

"We have to trust Beach Head," you tell Leatherneck. "Quick—switch the headphones."

Zartan is speaking to the leader of his Crimson Guards. Dr. Mindbender's attention is on the dials and knobs he is turning on his control panel in preparation for zapping your brains. You take advantage of their distraction. You reach up and reverse the headphones.

"Hey—what're they doing?" a Crimson Guard cries as he sees you reversing the headphones.

Dr. Mindbender doesn't seem to hear him.

"Wait! Stop!" the Crimson Guard cries.

But Mindbender throws the switch....

Turn to page 62.

The Crimson Guards take you to Zartan's headquarters, a long, low building on the water's edge. As CGs shove you toward the main entry, you peer around to the back. You see a small dock with a speedboat tied to it. Beyond the dock, out on the ocean, a small COBRA battle cruiser is anchored.

Inside, the corridors are low and dark. You pass by several closed-off rooms. "That's the lab, Mindbender's lab," Beach Head whispers as you pass a closed wooden door.

"Shut up, scum!" a Crimson Guard yells, jamming the butt of his rifle hard into Beach Head's back. Beach Head doesn't utter a cry. He keeps walking as if the attack hadn't happened.

You are herded into a small, unfurnished chamber, dimly lit by electric torches on the wall. A few moments later Zartan enters, hooded, with black triangles painted around his eye. But even through the disguise, you can see that he is troubled by your appearance.

"I hate uninvited guests," he snarls, swirling his maroon cape around him. "Especially when an *invited* guest is due here any second." He thinks for a few moments, pacing the small chamber nervously.

"Aha! I have a wonderful plan! Let's go on a little boat ride, shall we?"

Turn to page 21.

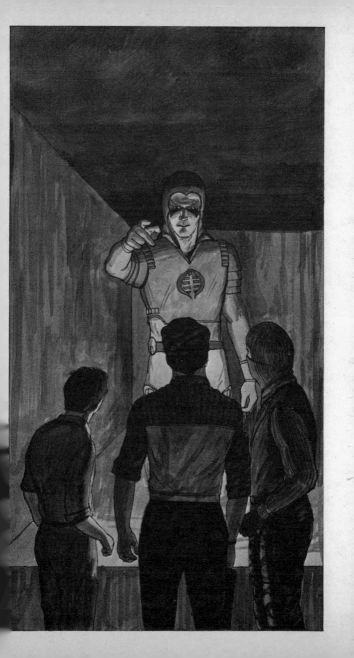

Both of you drop to the soft ground, your rifles gripped tightly, your eyes searching the thick foliage. A bird shrieks a warning above your heads. You ignore its shrill cry, keeping your eyes straight ahead as the sounds of approaching footsteps grow louder.

Suddenly, two figures appear a few yards ahead.

"Airtight! Beach Head!" you cry, leaping to your feet. "Over here!"

"Where've you guys been?" Leatherneck demands angrily. "You stop off at the country club for a swim?"

Your two comrades walk quickly toward you without replying. Their expressions are grim. Their eyes stare at you strangely. Have they found something up ahead?

"You guys see anything?" you ask.

"Yeah. I brought you something," Airtight says. "It's *this*!"

He pulls back his right arm and brings his fist forward with all his might against your chin.

Turn to page 13.

"AAAAIIIIII!" the Crimson Guards scream as they are struck and engulfed by a sizzling electronic ray.

The lights in the lab dim. The room grows silent. The machine is dead.

"Zartan is escaping! Let's get him! We cannot let him get away!" one of the Crimson Guards yells.

"Command us, sir, and we will obey," another CG says to you.

You realize at once that Dr. Mindbender's ray has made the CGs loyal to the G.I. Joe Team. You don't have time to think about this amazing turn of events, though. Suddenly, Zartan returns to the lab, dragging with him a struggling Dr. Mindbender!

Turn to page 15.

Dr. Mindbender begins to lift the chopper off the ground. It goes up slowly because of the heaviness of the weapons on board—four rockets and a negator bomb, in addition to the 30-millimeter cannon on the front.

You run underneath the chopper and leap up. You grab the runners and hold on for dear life. Mindbender must realize what you have done. He begins to swerve the chopper, maneuvering it forward, then quickly back.

You look down. The island is far below you now. "What on earth am I doing here?" you ask yourself. But you realize you're not in a position to change your mind. It's hard to breathe. The wind rushes at you like a tornado.

You close your eyes and try to pull yourself up to the cockpit. Mindbender swerves, dives, and cuts, trying to throw you off.

Up and up you pull yourself, clinging to the side of the COBRA chopper like an ant walking up a kitchen wall.

Using every ounce of strength you possess, you pull yourself up to the small cockpit—

—and stare straight into the barrel of Mindbender's pistol.

Turn to page 22.

"I'm comin', Hawk!" you yell as you lunge toward him.

But Monkeywrench blocks your way. He raises his length of chain and swings it around your neck.

You gasp for breath. He's cut off your air supply. Furiously, you tear at the chain, pull yourself free, and dive toward Hawk. But Monkeywrench isn't finished with you. He sticks out a big boot and trips you. The chain comes swinging down again.

You roll out of the way, and it misses. You barrel into Zartan's midsection. He cries out in surprise and drops his machine rifle. You dive for the weapon—

—but Hawk dives for it too.

Was the switch thrown? Did Dr. Mindbender's loyalty ray shoot through Hawk's brain before you could get to him?

Hawk pulls off the headphones and aims the machine rifle at your chest. "Another victory for the glorious Zartan!" he yells.

Everyone turns to watch Hawk as he holds the rifle to your chest and prepares to fire....

Turn to page 39.

55

You decide to wait it out. You've got to find out what's going on here.

"Take them to Dr. Mindbender's lab!" Zartan commands.

You are shoved through a door, into a vast room, filled from floor to ceiling with electronic machinery and wiring. Dr. Mindbender enters the lab wearing a white lab coat. He is short and bald, but his unnerving stare lets you know right away that he is a powerful and evil man. Zartan must have paid him a great deal to coax him away from COBRA Commander, you tell yourself.

"Ah, new recruits," he says quietly. "Let's hook them up and see if we can make good boys of them." He laughs at his little joke.

You and Leatherneck are dragged over to a large console. Headphones are placed over your ears. "What are you doing, Mindbender?" you demand.

"It's quite simple, really," answers COBRA's mad scientist. "So simple even a G.I. Joe idiot can understand it, I believe. I'm going to transmit some rays into your brain, that's all. I call them loyalty rays. When I'm finished, you will be as loyal to Zartan as your two buddies."

"Soon *everyone* will be loyal to me!" Zartan cries. You realize that he has been watching the entire procedure. "Even COBRA Commander will be loyal to me—and I will control all of COBRA Command!"

Go on to page 57.

Dr. Mindbender, a wide smile beneath his thick, black mustache, walks over to confer with Zartan. While they talk in a corner of the long laboratory, Beach Head makes his way over to the console. He talks with one of the CGs standing guard and then comes over to you.

"Listen, there's only one way to save yourselves," he whispers to you and Leatherneck. You struggle to hear his whispering through the heavy headphones.

"You can reverse the effect of the ray. Just turn the headphones around—quickly. Put the right headphone on your left ear, the left headphone on your right ear."

Leatherneck looks at him skeptically.

"I'm telling you—it'll work. It'll save you!" Beach Head whispers.

Leatherneck turns to you with a scowl. "We can't trust him. He's a traitor," he mutters.

You don't know whether or not to trust Beach Head and reverse the headphones. But you know you have to act quickly. Dr. Mindbender is heading for his control panel. What will you do?

Trust your old pal and turn the headphones around to save yourselves? Turn to page 49.

Try to free yourselves before the rays are activated? Turn to page 66.

Flint, Roadblock, and the infantrymen disappear into the trees. They will make their way through the forest and wait outside Zartan's headquarters in case your plan to trick Zartan runs into problems.

Airtight and Beach Head train their rifles on you as you and Leatherneck, your hands loosely tied behind you, walk ahead of them. The afternoon sun is low in the sky, but the heat hasn't lessened, and you are all dripping with sweat as you arrive at the low structure on the edge of the water—Zartan's secret headquarters.

"Now, remember to act a little dazed and weird," you tell your two captors.

"That won't be hard for Airtight!" Leatherneck mumbles.

"Once we're inside, we'll wait to catch Zartan off-guard," you say, a little nervous. You don't like facing an enemy with your hands tied behind you.

"Halt!" a voice cries from behind you.

A unit of COBRA Crimson Guards steps forward, their rifles trained on you.

"I've brought Zartan some new recruits," Airtight tells them.

The CGs do not hesitate. "Follow us," the leader says....

Go on to page 59.

The CGs march you into a long, low chamber, dimly lit by electric torches on two walls. They move to take away the rifles from Beach Head and Airtight, but the two G.I. Joe Team members pull away.

"Hey—what's the idea?" Airtight yells. "We're on *your* side now—did you forget?"

"Hand over your rifles. The Guards are acting on *my* orders!" a shrill, high-pitched voice calls.

You turn and look into the grinning face of Zartan!

His face is painted white with large black triangles over his eyes. His lips are also black. He has never been seen without a disguise of some sort.

"We—uh—brought in these prisoners, sir," Airtight says.

"Shut up, fool!" Zartan yells angrily, his black lips twisting into an ugly frown. He holds up a small radio receiver. "You G.I. Joe clowns underestimate me. Your little trick is pathetic. Did you really think I wouldn't have those three imbecile Dreadnoks wired? With my little radio receiver here, I heard every word that was spoken. You have tricked only yourselves."

You pull your hands free and start to run to the door. But you are immediately grabbed by Crimson Guards, who throw you to the floor.

"Take them to Dr. Mindbender!" Zartan commands. "I'll show them a *real* trick!"

Turn to page 14.

"We don't need tricks!" Leatherneck yells. "*This* is all we need!" He raises his trusty M-1 high in the air.

"Throw him some raw meat and he'll settle down," Airtight says.

"Leatherneck is right," you decide. "Come on, guys—let's go get 'em!"

"YO, JOE!" is the cry as you and Flint lead the rest of the G.I. Joe unit through the tangled trees toward Zartan's island headquarters.

KA-ZOW! KA-ZOW! KA-ZOWKA-ZOW!

You hit the ground behind some low bushes as COBRA Crimson Guards begin to fire at you. The CGs are positioned behind a low fence built of white logs. Beyond the fence stands Zartan's fortress. To the side of the low, wooden fortress you see a dock with a small powerboat tied to it.

"We don't have time for games with these clowns in the red monkey suits!" you yell. You stand up and lob a grenade at the low, white fence.

The fence is blown apart in a fiery blast of blinding whites and yellows. Most of the CGs are blown away. Your rifle fire takes care of those that remain.

"C'mon—we're goin' in!" you cry.

Turn to page 4.

You feel a sharp tingle as the rays penetrate your brain. Your whole body feels as if it is vibrating. Bright colors flash before your eyes. Then everything goes white....

When you regain consciousness, you see that Zartan and Dr. Mindbender are having a good laugh with Beach Head. "You told them what?" Mindbender is saying. "Hahaha! And they *believed* you?" He slaps Beach Head on the back.

You laugh too. It was a funny joke for Beach Head to pull on you and Leatherneck. Now that you are on the same side you can appreciate a good joke like that one.

You salute your leader, Zartan, as he walks by, still smiling and shaking his head.

A Crimson Guard walks over to you. He hands a COBRA sniper rifle to each of you. "Other G.I. Joe units will be coming to this island soon to challenge us," he says grimly.

You and Leatherneck smile. "We can't wait," you say, raising your new rifles high.

THE END

Zartan confers with the COBRA ship captain. Then he summons the guards to give them instructions about COBRA Commander's arrival. You and your teammates take advantage of his activities to try and come up with a plan.

"The way I see it, we have two choices," you whisper to your pals. "It isn't far to shore. We could jump overboard and swim back to Zartan's headquarters. Then maybe we could wait somewhere, warn COBRA Commander of Zartan's plot, and let COBRA Commander fight it out with Zartan. And while Zartan and COBRA Commander are busy, we destroy Mindbender's machine."

"I ain't in that much of a mood for a swim," Leatherneck says, looking down at the choppy waters. "What's your other plan?"

"We could try to grab control of this battle cruiser," you say.

The CGs are returning. You realize you must decide which plan to put into effect—at once!

Jump overboard and head back to Zartan's headquarters? Turn to page 75.

Try to take control of the battle cruiser? Turn to page 16.

63

Timing your jump perfectly, you leap off the battleship and hit the water in front of one of the WHALES. Seconds later, you are being pulled onto the small craft by Shipwreck.

"Hey, the fishin' is pretty good down here," he says with a grin. "Hawk thought you might need a little company, since you were too busy to report in these last few hours."

"The more, the merrier," you tell him. "Who's that over there with the trusty laser rifle? Hey—Sci-Fi—it's you!"

Sci-Fi gives you a slow smile. He does everything slowly. It's part of his training. You've got to be slow and steady when you're handling laser weaponry.

"Sci-Fi, how about a small favor?" you ask, smiling back. "Think you can knock out that long, low building on the shore?"

Turn to page 85.

"Airtight—is that you? Stop bumping me!" you cry, struggling to keep up your fast pace through the choppy waters.

Then, to your left, about twenty yards away, you see Airtight. Who—or what—is bumping your legs, bouncing against your back? Airtight suddenly stops swimming, throws up his hands. You see a look of horror cross his face. He tries to scream.

"Sharks! Sharks!" you hear Leatherneck cry from behind you.

You feel a paralyzing stab of pain in your right leg. You spin in the water, whirl around to face your attacker. You are surrounded. The water is filled with sharks—*hungry* sharks!

What has attracted so many hungry sharks to these shallow waters? You figure that perhaps the electronic rays pouring from Dr. Mindbender's lab have drawn these deadly foes.

But, sadly, you won't have time to prove your theory. Your open-jawed attackers close in on you. The sharks cannot believe their good fortune. They've been waiting so long for company to drop in for dinner....

THE END

You look into Beach Head's eyes. You cannot tell whether the effect of the ray has worn off or not. "Sorry, Beach Head," you say quietly. You look up to see Dr. Mindbender working methodically at the control panel.

He is about to throw the master switch.

You nod your head in signal to Leatherneck, and the two of you lunge forward, ripping the headphones from the console. You shove Beach Head out of the way and heave the headphones at Dr. Mindbender.

He ducks in surprise and stumbles backward.

"Stop them! Stop them!" Zartan shrieks. He runs from the lab to summon reinforcements.

The Crimson Guards, startled at first, regain their composure. They charge toward you and Leatherneck, ready for a fight....

Turn to page 34.

You carefully aim your rifle at the chopper. *BAAAARRRROOOOOOOOM!*

No one should ever shoot at a COBRA F.A.N.G.

In addition to the four rockets it carries, it is also armed with a powerful negator bomb, which you set off by shooting your rifle.

Oh, well. You can't say this adventure didn't end with a *bang*!

THE END

BAAARRRROOOOOM!

The boat was a trap, rigged with explosives.

Your hopes of capturing Zartan are blown sky-high.

And so are you.

THE END

The ropes fall away from Hawk and Lady Jaye. They were never really tied up. They are both smiling.

Zartan suddenly steps forward, and the laughter stops. "Seize them!" he cries. Crimson Guards rush forward to do his bidding. "Your precious Hawk and Lady Jaye are thousands of miles away! You have thrown away your weapons—and your chances—for imposters!"

You dive to the ground and try to retrieve your rifle, but a CG kicks it across the floor, and two other CGs pounce on you. Your comrades try to put up a fight, but they are quickly subdued.

Turn to page 87.

"Let's mow 'em down!" Leatherneck says, ready to fire.

"Let 'em rip," you tell him grimly.

"Wait!" says Beach Head. "Let them get a little closer. Why give 'em a chance to turn tail and ride back to warn Zartan?"

You've got another fast decision to make, Commando. Shoot now and take the Dreadnoks by surprise? Or wait until they're closer and easier to ambush? Decide quickly—they're roaring over the soft ground and will be on top of you in seconds!

Shoot now? Turn to page 83.
Wait till they're closer? Turn to page 36.

"Zartan's getting away!" Airtight yells.

"He won't get far," you say, your eyes on the giant electronic console. "He's activated this machine. We'd better take care of it first."

"Leave it to me," Leatherneck snaps. He raises his M-1 and begins blasting away at the console. Sparks crackle. The metal bends. Pieces fly off.

Zartan's Crimson Guards burst into the room. Leatherneck blasts away. "Duck down!" you yell. "It's going to explode!"

You hit the floor just as the machine blows up in a fiery burst of oranges and yellows. The room vibrates with electricity. Jagged, bright yellow rays—like bolts of lightning—zigzag across the lab.

Turn to page 53.

71

"Lady Jaye doesn't beg, and Hawk would never command us to surrender," you tell your teammates. "Keep up the attack!"

Zartan ducks to the floor as you and your comrades raise your rifles and begin firing at the surprised Crimson Guards. Hawk and Lady Jaye, tossing off the ropes that tied them, begin running toward the large red door at the back of the chamber. As they run, they tug at their faces—and pull away holographic masks! You realize you have made the correct decision to keep fighting. These two fleeing imposters are not Hawk and Lady Jaye—they are Zarana and Zandar, masters of disguise, attempting to help out their brother Zartan.

The roar of the rifle fire is deafening. Zartan follows his brother and sister through the red door. "Don't let them get away!" you cry.

Followed by Airtight, Beach Head, Flint, and the others, you blast your way through the red door and charge into the next room. The room is filled from floor to ceiling with machinery and wiring. You have found Dr. Mindbender's lab! Zartan feverishly spins some dials and throws a switch on the largest console. Then he runs from the room.

What is this machine? Should you take the time to shut it off—and risk letting Zartan escape? Or should you go after Zartan right away?

Chase after him? Turn to page 29.
Turn off the machine first? Turn to page 71.

72

"Aha!" Dr. Mindbender yells gleefully as he throws the switch. He turns to watch you squirm as his machine's electronic rays flow into your brain.

You close your eyes.

But you don't feel anything. And you don't hear anything. And you don't feel any different.

When you open your eyes, you see that Mindbender is staring at you in horror. "What went wrong? Why didn't it work?" he screams, pounding furiously on the control panel, throwing the switch again and again.

The four of you take advantage of his confusion. With a burst of muscle power, you pull yourselves free from the machine. Before the stunned Crimson Guards can move, you rush forward, grab Dr. Mindbender, and take him prisoner.

"Shoot them! Don't let them get away!" the CG leader yells, raising his rifle.

BLAM! BLAM! BLAM! BLAM! BLAM-BLAMBLAMBLAM!

Turn to page 40.

"Okay, swim time," you whisper to your comrades.

You look over at Zartan, who is still talking excitedly to the battleship captain. Both of them, you see, are unarmed. That means that only the three guards stand between you and the water.

Two of the guards are standing with their backs to you as they stare up at the rolling pinks and purples of the spectacular sunset. The third Crimson Guard stares suspiciously at the four of you, his hand resting on the holster of his automatic pistol.

You stare back at him, your mind racing through plan after plan. Finally, you decide to try one of the oldest tricks in the book. You point up into the sky behind the CG. "Wow! I don't believe that!" you yell.

Will he fall for it?

Yes. He turns away for just an instant.

It's all the time you need. You barrel into him. He cries out as you knock him to the deck. Airtight slams another CG against the side of the ship. Leatherneck picks up the third CG and heaves him overboard.

"Stop! Stop, you fools!" Zartan screams. But he is powerless to stop you now.

All four of you climb over the low rail. You hit the water with a loud splash. The shock of the sudden cold paralyzes you for just an instant. And then you are swimming, swimming with fast, furious strokes toward the shore.

Turn to page 65.

"You guys have had it," Airtight says, still looking dazed. "Zartan will be here to rescue us soon."

Zartan? What does COBRA's master of disguise have to do with this?

"Let's drag them back into the trees, where it's safer," you tell Leatherneck. "Maybe they'll snap out of it."

"Back in 'Nam, guys would go crazy sometimes," Leatherneck says, dragging Beach Head by the feet. "But I never seen anything to beat this."

"Zartan is our leader now," Airtight says quietly.

You deposit both of them in the shade of a sprawling old palm tree, its broad, jagged leaves forming a protective umbrella above them.

But there is no protection for you on the ground. You turn and see that you are surrounded by COBRA Crimson Guards!

Turn to page 17.

76

Zartan is on the dock now. His boots clatter over the hard wooden planks. Leatherneck raises his rifle, but he's running too hard to aim accurately. His shots fly over Zartan's head.

Zartan reaches the end of the small dock. He disappears. "Hurry—he's in the boat!" you yell. You and Leatherneck run over the sand, reach the dock, keep running to the end.

Gasping for breath, you reach the end of the dock and look into the small powerboat. Zartan isn't on it....

Turn to page 38.

Headphones are placed over your ears. Mindbender ambles over to a control panel. Humming quietly to himself, he turns knobs, adjusts switches.

You realize that your only chance is to be rescued once again by Flint, Roadblock, and the other soldiers. But what is keeping them? They should have been bursting in with their guns blazing by now.

Still humming, Dr. Mindbender reaches for the master switch.

"Flint—where are you? Where are you guys?" you say to yourself, staring as Dr. Mindbender grabs the switch....

...and pulls it!

Turn to page 74.

"Let's get Mindbender!" you yell to Leatherneck over the roar of rifle fire. "He's the key to the operation here!"

"Look at the coward try to run," Leatherneck says, his mouth twisted in disgust as you both watch Mindbender keeping to the shadows, slowly crawling toward the doorway. "Let's go weasel huntin'!" Leatherneck yells.

The two of you charge right through the Crimson Guards, using your rifles as battering rams. "Think you can hold 'em off while we go after Mindbender?" you call to Airtight.

"Does Abe Lincoln have fleas?" he calls back.

You realize that his reply makes no sense at all—but you have no choice. You leave Airtight and Beach Head to battle the CGs, and you and Leatherneck take off after Mindbender.

Mindbender makes it through the doorway. You pursue him down a long, dark corridor, ducking your head because of the low ceiling. He reaches the exit of the building when he suddenly turns and fires a small pistol at you.

The bullets whistle through the dark hallway, taking you by surprise. You didn't know he was armed.

You hear a deep groan. Leatherneck's been hit!

Turn to page 45.

79

"Lead us back to Zartan's headquarters," you tell Airtight and Beach Head, "if you're both feeling okay now."

"We're okay," Airtight mutters, climbing to his feet. "We didn't get a full dose of the ray. There was a problem with Mindbender's machine. I guess that's why the effect wasn't permanent."

The sun rests lower in the afternoon sky, but the air is still hot and steamy as you cut your way through the tall vines and tangled trees.

As you reach a small, circular clearing, you hear a sound—a low roar that's getting louder. "Hit the dirt!" you yell. Peering through the tall weeds, you see three motorcycles roaring over the marshy ground, rapidly closing in. And riding these powerful choppers are three thugs you immediately recognize—Ripper, Buzzer, and Monkeywrench—the Dreadnoks!

"Let's blast these bums!" cries Leatherneck, leaping to his feet and raising the big M1 to his shoulder.

"No, wait!" cries Airtight. "Let's play a little trick on these louts instead! They're easy to outsmart. Let's tell 'em we've all been zapped by Dr. Mindbender's machine, and we're just as loyal to Zartan as they are! Then they can lead us right into Zartan's fortress."

Which will it be, Commando—blast 'em or try to trick 'em?

Blast 'em? Turn to page 70.
Trick 'em? Turn to page 32.

80

You drop and swerve, dodging incoming weaponfire. Suddenly the radio comes to life. "Anybody here call for help? We were in the neighborhood. Thought we'd join the party."

Suddenly, there's a barrage of sound, followed by the most beautiful sight you've ever seen—a squadron of Skystriker fighter jets!

It must look like the Fourth of July from below, you think. But this is no fireworks show —it's deadly serious. A few minutes later, all that remains of the COBRA Rattlers are wispy trails of black smoke in the sky.

"YO, JOE!" you yell happily.

Back at the Pit, a grim-faced Hawk shakes your hand. "A close call," he says quietly. "Sorry I missed the air show."

"What about Airtight and Beach Head?" you ask.

"They made it out," Hawk says. "But they had to blow up the entire island to get away."

"Had to blow up the *entire island*?" you ask.

"You know those guys," Hawk says. "They'd blow up their grandmothers if it would make an exciting end to a mission!"

"Well, I still think it was a little sloppy of them," you say, grinning.

"Luckily," says Hawk, "in a mission like this, neatness doesn't count!"

You nod your head in agreement, breathe a sigh of relief that the mission is over, and head off to get some needed R & R.

THE END

You nod to Leatherneck, and his M-1 lets go with a deadly barrage of .45-caliber weapon-fire. All four of you begin to fire at the approaching Dreadnoks.

They wheel up in surprise. Their choppers spin out from under them, stirring up a wall of thick sand and dust.

You keep firing even though you can't see them. When the dust begins to clear, you see too clearly that you have made a tactical mistake.

The Dreadnoks are armed with *grenades*!

You and your three team members hit the ground. But the weeds of the clearing don't provide much cover.

The adventure has an explosive finish. Unfortunately, *you're* the target of the explosives! Your chances of getting to Zartan have gone to pieces. And so, Commando, have you.

THE END

Before you can stop him, Zartan hits Leatherneck again. You dive for Zartan and realize you have another problem—Zandar's pistol is pointed straight at you. You make a grab for the pistol, but Zandar jerks it away.

Leatherneck lies unconscious on the pavement.

You stare down at him angrily. Your anger drives you forward. You slam into Zandar just as he pulls the trigger. The bullet whistles past you, and he topples over backward. You pull yourself up and make a diving tackle at Zartan. He steps easily away.

You look up. What is that sound?

The sky is filled with planes. The ground seems to shake from the thunderous jets. COBRA Rattlers!

Zartan and Zandar take cover underneath the Skystriker as the Rattlers begin to riddle the airstrip with combat rockets and cluster bombs. There's no shelter for you and your friend.

You and Leatherneck have kept them from finding the Pit—but COBRA has won this round. Your adventure ends here, Commando, on this lonely airstrip in the green, rolling hills of Pennsylvania.

THE END

"Mebbe," Sci-Fi says, taking careful aim, slowly positioning the laser rifle. "Hold 'er steady, Shipwreck, and I'll give you a little demo of laser technology."

Shipwreck struggles to keep the WHALE steady in the tossing waters.

"Steady...steady...steady...*BLAAAAAA-AAAAAAAM!*"

Zartan's headquarters explodes in a wall of flame. Dr. Mindbender's transmitter is melted along with everything else.

"Well...that about wraps up our job here. Nice shootin', Sci-Fi," you tell him.

"You don't know how nice," he says slowly, his voice cracking. "*You* try firing a laser rifle when you're as seasick as I am!"

THE END

Leatherneck swats a mosquito and scowls, perspiration pouring off his thick mustache. You can see that he is impatient to get moving. But you want to hear the rest of Beach Head's story first.

"Zartan isn't alone here," Beach Head tells you. "He has this scientist working with him, a Dr. Mindbender. We overheard a conversation. It seems that Mindbender isn't loyal to COBRA Commander anymore, either. He's workin' with Zartan. They've got something cooked up to make Zartan the big leader of everything."

"We'll see about that!" Leatherneck growls.

"They hooked Airtight and me up to a big machine in this lab that Mindbender has built. They put headphones on us and—zap!—transmitted some kind of rays into us."

"And the rays made you forget who you were?" you ask eagerly.

"No, not that," Beach Head says, trying to remember exactly what it was like. "We felt... we felt—"

"Loyal to Zartan," Airtight finishes his sentence for him. "Dr. Mindbender's machine made us feel total loyalty to that miserable little chameleon."

"Well, ya know what I think?" Leatherneck interrupts, packing up the supplies. "I think that a chameleon ain't nothin' but a lizard! Let's go stomp on him!"

Turn to page 80.

86

Looking up, you see the two figures you believed to be Hawk and Lady Jaye removing holographic masks, still grinning, still celebrating their triumph. You recognize them immediately as Zandar and Zarana, Zartan's brother and sister, also masters of disguise. They toss their disguises to the floor, give their brother Zartan a quick salute, turn, and leave the room.

"Take them to Dr. Mindbender," Zartan orders his Crimson Guards. "He will make loyal soldiers of them. Too bad his machine can't also make them smarter! Hahaha!"

With Zartan's laughter ringing in your ears, you are led to the chamber of Dr. Mindbender. The door swings open, and you walk slowly—into a darkness that will never lift. . . .

THE END

"What kept ya?" Leatherneck turns his head as you stagger in, breathing hard, exhausted, chilled, and wet.

His M-1 is trained on a crowd of Crimson Guards—and Zartan. Leatherneck seems to have captured them all—one-handed.

"You told me not to do this, so I had to do it," he explains.

"I'm glad you didn't listen to me for a change," you tell him.

"Looks like you been for a swim," he says, sneering.

"I like to get my exercise in," you tell him. "You know, I may have to have words with you about disobeying my orders."

"There are only two words I want to hear," Leatherneck says.

"I bet I know what they are," you say, beating him to it. "MISSION ACCOMPLISHED."

THE END

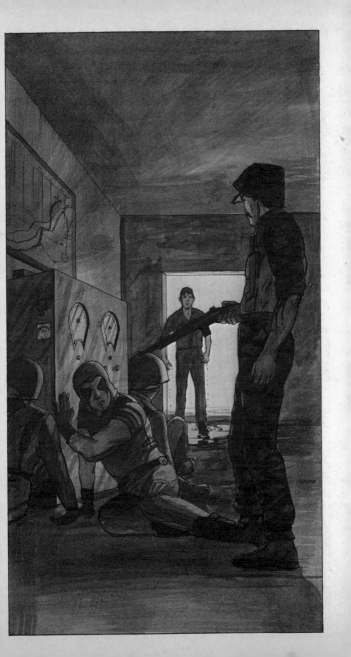